W9-BTD-282

Hello Kitty

Hello World!

illustrated by Higashi Glaser

HARRY N. ABRAMS, INC., PUBLISHERS

Hello Kitty®

Hello Mama & Papa!

I am off to see the world! I have packed my clothes and guidebook, dressed teddy, and gathered the addresses of all my friends. I will write to all of you when I arrive in each country.

Many languages are spoken around the world. So I have learned how to say "hello" in the language of each country I will visit. It is nice to say "hello" to someone in their own language even if that is the only word you know! I can look up other foreign words in my guidebook and learn how to pronounce them in the languages as well.

As you can imagine, I am very excited. The plane is ready. I'm off!

Love, Hello Kitty

© 1976, 2000 Sanrio Co., Ltd. Used under license

to: Mama & Papa
London, England

Sanrio smiles

kangaroo
Ayers Rock
koala
barbecue
wombat
Tasmanian devil
emu
dingo
Australia

G'day Australia!

Alô Brazil!
cacao tree
Sugar Loaf Mountain
Rio de Janeiro
mask
fruit
Carnival
jaguar
pipoca
costume
pink popcorn
Brazil

rain forest
tamarin
toucan
macaws
boa constrictor
canoe
arrow-poison frog
caiman

Ni hao China!

lantern
calligraphy
potstickers
dumplings
noodles
dragon
ricksha

kite
panda
The Great Wall
bamboo
tangerine
China

Marhaba Egypt!

Pyramids of Giza

The Great Sphinx

mummy

veil

Nile River

mosque
date tree
market
camel
dates
coriander
saffron
cumin
vessel

Bonjour France!
flag
Arc de Triomphe
Eiffel Tower
beret
cars
baguette
France

Haute Couture
hat
boutique
bonbon
milk
croissant
pastries
grapes
petit fours
cow
cheese

Namaste India!

cobra

sari

Bengal tiger

elephant

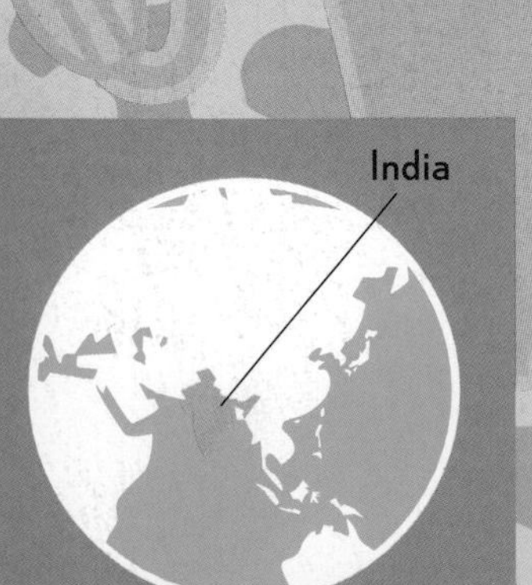

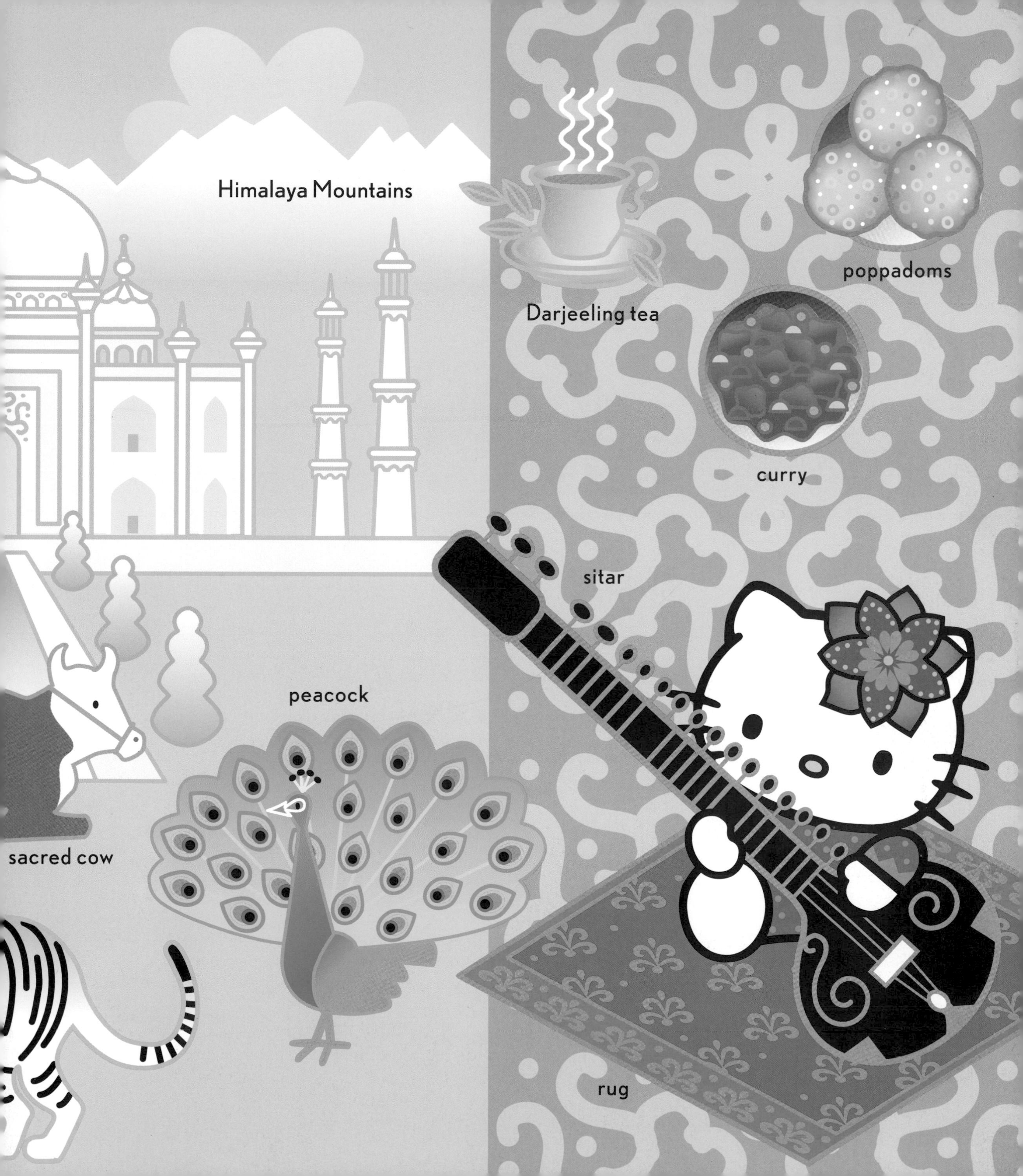
Himalaya Mountains
Darjeeling tea
poppadoms
curry
sitar
peacock
sacred cow
rug

Dia dhuit Ireland!

Cliffs of Moher

Giant's Causeway

gannet

puffin

steeplechase

Ireland

shamrock

Rock of Cashel
Blarney Castle
cottage
sheep
accordion
harp
fiddle
jig
tin whistle

Buon giorno Italy!

penne
rigatoni
ravioli
salami
art
spaghetti
gnocchi
ruoti
cappelletti
tortellini
cappuccino
gelato
purse
farfalle
rigate
boot
stiletto
shoe
fusilli

Kon'nichi wa Japan!

sushi roll

shrimp sushi

bonsai

kimono

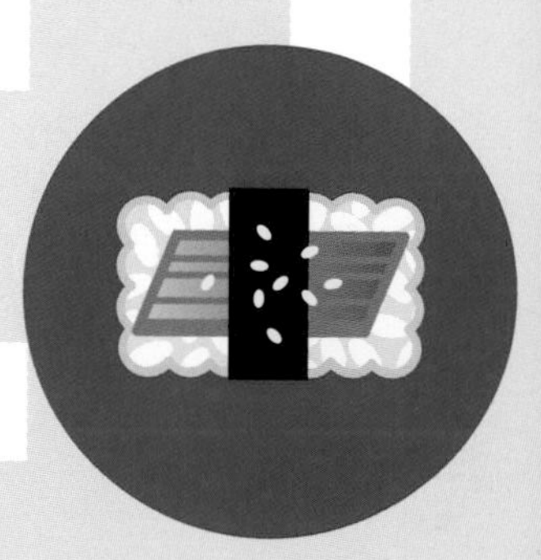

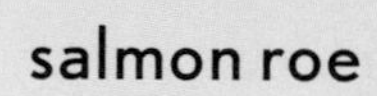

salmon roe

eel sushi

tuna sushi

origami
Mount Fuji
macaque
parasol
torii
koi fish
rock garden
taiko drum
cherry blossoms
Japan

Jambo Kenya!

giraffes
huts
baobab tree
rhinoceros
water
savanna
Kenya

Hola Mexico!

marigolds

Day of the Dead

Privet Russia!

chess

Fabergé egg

blinis

caviar

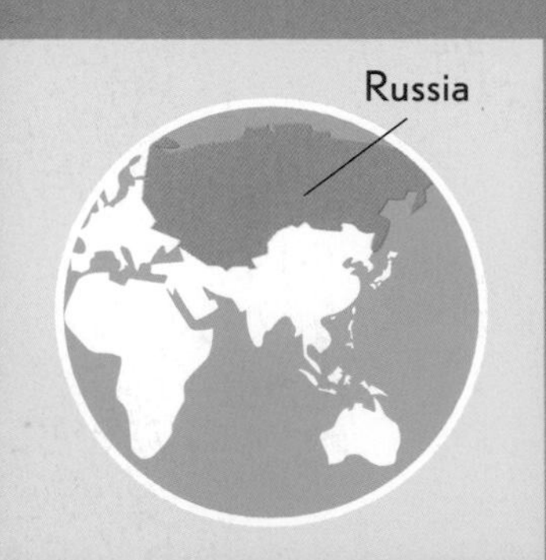

ballet
spruce tree
brown bear
Saint Basil's Cathedral
matreshka

Hello USA!

West
Grand Canyon
cowgirl
Golden Gate Bridge
hamburger
HOLLYWOOD
convertible car
corn

hot dog
North
lighthouse
Gateway Arch
Midwest
lobster
Empire State Building
East
Statue of Liberty
dolphins
cattle
oranges
river boat
baseball
USA
jazz
South

Translation Guide

Australia English

Australia Australia (aw-'strayl-yuh)
Ayers Rock Uluru ('oo-loo-roo)
barbecue barbie ('bah-bee)
dingo dingo ('ding-goe)
emu emu ('ee-mew)
Great Barrier Reef Great Barrier Reef (great 'bah-ree-ah reef)
Harbour Bridge Harbour Bridge ('hah-buh bridge)
hello g'day (g-'dey)
kangaroo kangaroo (kang-'ga-roo)
koala koala (koo-'wah-luh)
Opera House Opera House ('op-rah house)
Sydney to Hobart Yacht Race Sydney to Hobart Yacht Race ('sid-nee tuh 'hoe-baht yoht race)
Tasmanian devil Tasmanian devil (tas-mayn-ee-an deh-vul)
wombat wombat ('wom-bat)

Brazil Portuguese

arrow-poison frog sapo venenoso ('sah-poh veh-neh-'noh-soh)
boa boa ('boh-ah)
Brazil Brasil (brah-'zee-oo)
cacao tree árvore de cacau ('ar-voor-reh day kah-'kah-oh)
caiman caimão (kay-'mah-oh)
canoe canoa (kah-'noh-ah)
Carnival Carnaval (kar-nah-'vahl)
costume fantasia (fahn-tah-'zee-ah)
fruit frutas ('froo-tahs)
hello alô (ah-'loh)
jaguar jaguar (jhag-'huar)
macaws araras (ah-'rah-rahs)
mask máscara ('mah-skah-rah)
pink popcorn pipoca cor de rosa (pee-'poh-kah kor day 'haw-sah)
rain forest floresta tropical (flor-'ehs-tah tro-pee-'kahl)
Rio de Janeiro Rio de Janeiro ('ree-oh day jhah-'neh-roh)
Sugar Loaf Mountain Pão de Açúcar (pah-oh day ah-'zoo-khar)
tamarin tamarindo (tah-mah-'reen-doh)
toucan tucano (too-'kah-noh)

China Chinese

bamboo zhuzi (joo-dz)
calligraphy kaishu (kie-shoo)
China Zhongguo (jung-gwoh)
dragon long (lung)
dumplings jiaozi (jyow-dz)
The Great Wall Chang Cheng (chahng chung)
hello nihao (nee-how)
kite fengzheng (fung-jung)
lantern denglong (dung-lung)
noodles mien (myen)
panda xiongmao (shyung-mao)
potstickers guotieh (gwoh-tyeh)
ricksha san lun chee (saan lwun chuh)
tangerine juzi (jyoo-dz)

Egypt Arabic

camel jæmæl ('je-mel)
coriander kuzbara ('kooz-ba-ra)
cumin kammoon (kam-'moon)
date tree shajarat bælæh ('sha-ja-rat 'beh-leh)
dates bælæh ('beh-leh)
Egypt Misr ('mis-ur)
The Great Sphinx Abou el Hole ('a-boo el hole)
hello marhaba ('mar-ha-ba)
market suq (sook)
mosque jameah ('jem-may-ah)
mummy moumia ('moo-meea)
Nile River Nahr al Niel ('na-her el neel)
Pyramids of Giza Ahrram el Giza (a-huh-rham el 'gee-z
saffron zæfraan (za-'a fa-'ran)
veil nekab ('neh-kahb)
vessel waæeh (wa-'eh)

France French

Arc de Triomphe L'arc de triomphe (lark duh tree-'umf)
baguette baguette (bah-'get)
beret béret (beh-'reh)
bonbon bonbon (bohn-bohn)
boutique boutique (boo-'teek)
cars les autos (lay-'soh-toh)
cheese fromage (froh-'majh)
cow vache (vahsh)
croissant croissant (kwa-'sant)
Eiffel Tower La tour Eiffel (la too eff-'el)
flag drapeau ('drah-poh)

France France (frahns)
grapes raisins (ray-'sah)
hat chapeau (shah-'poh)
hello bonjour (bohn joor)
haute couture haute couture (ot coo-'toor)
milk lait (lay)
pastries les pâtisseries (lay pah-tis-er-'ee)
petit fours petits-fours (peh-tee-fur)

India Hindi

Bengal tiger Bengali baagh (bung-gaali baagh)
cobra cobra saap (co-abra saap)
curry curry (koo-ree)
Darjeeling tea Darjeeling chai (dar-'jee-ling chai)
elephant hathi (ha-a-thi)
hello namaste (nah-mas-tey)
Himalaya Mountains Himalay pahad (him-'ah-luy puh-'hud)
India Hindustan (hin-doo-stan)
peacock moar (mo-ar)
poppadoms poppadoms (pop-paa-doms)
rug chatai (chah-taa-ee)
sacred cow gaumata (gow-maata)
sari sari (saa-ree)
sitar sitar (see-taar)
Taj Mahal Taj Mahal (taaj muh-hull)

Ireland Gaelic

accordion cairdin (kore-jean)
Blarney Castle Caisleán Bhlárnaí (koosh-lawn blar-nee)
Cliffs of Moher Ailltreacha Mhóthair (all-truck-ka mow-her)
cottage tigín (tih-geen)
fiddle fidil (fidge-jil)
gannet gainnéad (gann-age)
Giant's Causeway Clochán na bhFómhórach (kla-hawn nuh vor-mu-ruck)
harp cláirseach cheilteach (klahr-shuck kell-chuck)
hello dia dhuit (jee-ah gootch)
Ireland Eire (air-uh)
jig dansa céilí (dan-suh kay-lee)
puffin cánóg (con-ohg)
Rock of Cashel Carraig Chaisil (car-rig kah-shil)
shamrock seamróg (sham-rogue)
sheep caora (kwee-rah)
steeplechase réis marchíocht (raysh mar-kee-oct)
tin whistle feadóg stáin (fah-dohj stahn)

Italy Italian

art arte ('ar-the)
boot stivale (stee-'vah-lay)
cappelletti cappelletti (kah-peh-'leh-tee)
cappuccino cappuccino (kah-poo-'chee-no)
Colosseum Colosseo (koh-loh-'say-oh)
farfalle farfalle (fahr-'fah-leh)
fusilli fusilli (foo-'see-lee)
gelato gelato (gel-'ah-toh)
gnocchi gnocchi ('nyo-kee)
gondola gondola ('gohn-doh-lah)
hello buon giorno (bohn 'jor-noh)
Italy Italia (ee-'tah-lee-ah)
Leaning Tower of Pisa Torre pendente di Pisa ('tor-ray dee 'pee-zah)
olive tree ulivo (oh-'lee-voh)
penne penne ('pen-neh)
purse borsa ('bohr-sah)
ravioli ravioli (rah-vee-'oh-lee)
Rialto Bridge Ponte Rialto ('pohn-tay ree-'ahl-toh)
rigate rigate (ree-'gah-tay)
rigatoni rigatoni (ree-'gah-'toh-nee)
ruoti ruote (roo-'oh-tay)
salami salame (sa-'lah-meh)
shoe scarpa ('skar-pah)
spaghetti spaghetti (spah-'get-tee)
stiletto tacho spilla ('ta-ko spee-lah)
tortellini tortellini (tor-teh-'lee-nee)

Japan Japanese

bonsai bonsai (bohn-sai)
cherry blossoms sakura (sa-koo-rah)
eel sushi anago (a-nah-goe)
hello kon'nichi wa (kon-'nee-chee-wa)
Japan Nihon (nee-hone)
kimono kimono (kee-mo-no)
koi fish koi (koi)
macaque nihon zaru (nee-hone za-roo)
Mount Fuji Fujisan (foo-jee san)
origami origami (o-ree-gah-mee)
parasol higasa (hee-gah-sah)
rock garden ganseki teien (gon-se-kee tay-en)
salmon roe ikura (ee-koo-rah)
shrimp sushi ebi (eh-bee)
sushi roll maki (ma-kee)
taiko drum taiko (tie-koh)
tuna sushi maguro zushi (ma-goo-roe zoo-shee)
torii torii (toh-ree)

Kenya Swahili

baobab tree mbuyu (um-'boo-yoo)
giraffes twiga ('twee-ga)
huts vibanda (vee-'bahn-da)
impalas swala ('swah-la)
Kenya Kenya ('ken-yah)
lion simba ('sim-ba)
Nairobi Nairobi (nai-'row-bee)
ngoma drum ngoma (ung-'go-ma)
rhinoceros kifaru (kee-'fa-roo)
savanna mbuga (um-'boo-ga)
water kisma (kee-'see-ma)
zebras pundamilia (poon-da-mee-'lee-ah)

Mexico Spanish

Baja Baja ('ba-ha)
bull toro ('toh-roh)
burrito burrito (boo-'ree-toh)
cactus nopal ('no-pal)
calacas calacas (kah-'lah-kas)
Day of the Dead El Día de los Muertos (el 'dee-ah day los 'mwer-tohs)
hello hola ('oh-lah)
mariachi mariachi (mah-ree-'ah-chee)
marigolds caléndulas (ka-'len-doo-las)
Metropolitan Cathedral Catedral Metropolitana (kah-te-'drahl meh-troh-poh-li-'tah-nah)
Mexico México ('may-hee-koh)
piñata piñata (pee-'nyah-tah)
sombrero sombrero (sohm-'breh-roh)
taco taco ('ta-koh)
Temple of the Moon Pirámide de la Luna (pee-'rah-mee-day day lah 'loo-nah)

Russia Russian

ballet balet (bah-'lyet)
blinis bliny (blee-'nuh)
brown bear buryi medved ('boo-ruhy med-'vyed)
caviar ikra (ee-'krah)
chess shakhmaty ('shah-mah-tuh)
Fabergé egg iaitso (yahy-'tsoh)
hello privet (pree-'vyet)
matreshka matreshka (mah-'tryoh-shkah)
Russia Rossiya (rah-see-ya)
spruce trees el (yel)
Saint Basil's Cathedral khram Vasiliia Blazhennogo ('hrahm vah-see-lee-yah blah-'gee-nah-vah)

Translations by TransPerfect Translations, Inc., New York

Library of Congress Catalog Card Number: 00-101111

ISBN 0-8109-3443-4

Hello Kitty® Characters, names, and all related indicia are trademarks of Sanrio Co., Ltd. Used under license.
© 1976, 2000 Sanrio Co., Ltd.

Published in 2000 by Harry N. Abrams, Incorporated, New York

All rights reserved. No part of the contents of this book may be reproduced without the written permission of the publisher.

Printed and bound in Hong Kong

Harry N. Abrams, Inc.
100 Fifth Avenue
New York, N.Y. 10011
www.abramsbooks.com